PUFFIN
THE MEETI

The animals of the jungle were Man was coming closer and closer to their naunts, chopping down the trees and burning them. Each night, beside the drinking pool (where no animal was allowed to kill, so that even the Ant-eater was forced to ignore the ants that ran to and fro across his feet), there were long discussions about how the Man and his destruction could be stopped. The Flying Fox, the Python, the Slow Loris, and Bruang the Bear all made suggestions, illustrating their ideas with a story. Together, these stories are a collection of witty, wise and delightful folk tales from Borneo, retold with a simplicity and humour that have preserved their place in children's literature.

First published in 1929, *The Meeting-Pool* has been republished many times. This edition includes the original illustrations drawn by R. W. Coulter.

For quite small children, for their elder brothers and sisters and for parents and grand-parents.

CONTENTS

THE MEETING-POOL

A TALE OF BORNEO

by

MERVYN • SKIPPER

WITH ILLUSTRATIONS

by

R.W. COULTER.

PENGUIN BOOKS

Puffin Books: a Division of Penguin Books Ltd,
Harmondsworth, Middlesex, England
Penguin Books Australia Ltd, Ringwood, Victoria, Australia
Penguin Books (N. Z.) Ltd, 182–190 Wairau Road, Auckland 10, New Zealand
Penguin Books Canada Ltd, 41 Steelcase Road, West Markham, Ontario, Canada

First published in 1929
First published in Puffin Books 1954
This edition first published 1975

Copyright © Estate of Mervyn Skipper, 1975

—

Filmset for Penguin Books Australia Ltd
by Asco Trade Typesetting Ltd, Hong Kong
Printed by Sheck Wah Tong Printing Press, Hong Kong

NOTE

The little island of Pulau Daat lies off the coast of the big island of Borneo. I do not think you will be able to find it on the map. It was on Pulau Daat that the writer collected the little stories in this book. He wrote them down for the amusement of his small daughter living in Australia, and they are now published in the hope that other children may find them entertaining.

THE
FIRST
MEETING

THE FIRST MEETING

AT WHICH IT IS DECIDED THAT THE WHITE MAN
MUST BE STOPPED

'WHY,' whimpered the Stick Insect, 'does the White Man want to steal our jungle?'

'Yes why?' squattered the Buffalo-leech, raising himself up on a leaf and waving his head to and fro. 'We haven't done him any harm.'

'Perhaps,' growled Bruang the Bear, looking out of his hole in the big tapang tree, 'perhaps he wants fresh meat. When he has cleared all the jungle he will certainly have plenty of that.'

All the animals with good flesh on their bones shivered and drew their tails, if they had any, between their legs. All except Babi the pig.

'When the last bit of jungle is cleared,' he squeaked, 'I shall swim across to Borneo.'

'*I* shall be waiting – then,' murmured the Crocodile, who had drawn himself up on the sand still hot from the sun which had just gone down. The other animals laughed, but not very cheerfully, and the pig drew back into the long grass, looking extremely sorry for himself.

It was the time when all the jungle creatures should have been out hunting, but now that the White Man was clearing away the jungle they felt too unhappy to hunt; so they had all come down to the meeting-pool, under the big tapang tree, to talk about it. A tiny stream ran out of the jungle into the sea, but just before it escaped into the ocean it rested for a moment in a little pool, a still, little pool that nestled under the red sea-cliff. It is the law of the island that no animal shall kill at the meeting-pool; and so the bee-eaters sat and looked hungrily at the bees, but did not dare to touch them, and Sang Nokdiak the Ant-eater nearly bit his long tongue off with vexation at the ants that ran to and fro over his feet.

Along a narrow spit of land behind the meeting-pool stretched the jungle, but it did not stretch very far. It was so thin and poorly now that when the animals went into it a little way they could see the blue sky shining between the tree trunks on every side, and if they went a little farther they could see the hills and valleys which had once been covered with forest but which were now bare and blackened with fire. Sometimes an animal, braver than the rest, would creep to the very edge of the jungle and looking out from amongst the leaves could see the White Man's coolies chopping down the trees, and sometimes they would see the White Man himself, in his white clothes with his big helmet on his head and a very red face, giving orders to the coolies in a very loud voice.

Every day the White Man sent his coolies to the edge of the very little bit of jungle that was left, and all day they chopped and chopped, and in the evening they would go away and come again the next day and chop down more trees; and then every few weeks the White Man put the red fire into the chopped-down trees and burnt them up.

'Well!' said the Stick Insect again, as all the jungle creatures sat silent looking into the meeting-pool. 'Nobody has been good enough to explain why the White Man wants to clear our jungle.'

'Perhaps he is looking for rare insects,' said the Ape.

'Or bezoar stones to make white magic with,' said the Stick Insect. The Ape looked foolish, for everybody knows he grows bezoar stones in his stomach.

'Rubbidge!' sang the Mosquito, who had buzzed up a moment before. 'None of you knows why the White Man clears the jungle. How could you! You stick to your jungle and you daren't poke your noses outside it. But I – I visit the White Man every night. I know!'

A shiver went through the grass and the leaves. All the birds and animals and insects were listening.

'The White Man cuts down the jungle,' went on the Mosquito, 'so that he can plant rubber-trees.'

A shout of laughter went up around the meeting-pool.

'Hok-hok,' said the Hornbill. 'My beak and feathers! Why should the White Man plant rubber-trees? There are plenty of rubber-trees in the jungle.'

'Because,' said the Mosquito, when he could make his thin voice heard, 'because any fool knows that a tame bullock does more work than a wild buffalo and a planted rubber-tree gives more sap than a wild one.'

'That's right,' said the King-crab, who had crept up out of the sea while the Mosquito was talking. 'I have been down to the west end and there are full-grown rubber-trees there, and every tree has a little cup tied round its waist and coolies come every day and make a cut in the bark for the sap to run into the cup, and women come afterwards and pour the sap from the cup into a bucket and take it away.'

'But what does the White Man want with the

stuff?' asked Rawa the big white pigeon. 'It looks like milk, but it is no good to eat. I have tried it, and it stuck my beak together so that I thought I would starve to death before I got it open again.'

'Yes,' said the Ape. 'What does he want with the stuff? Tell us that!'

'That I don't know,' said the Mosquito. 'He has it squeezed into thin sheets and sends it away to Labuan in boats, and there, so a wood-beetle who came over in a packing-case told me, it is put inside big steamers and carried to the other end of the world. What they do with it there I'm bothered if I know, but the White Man gets good money for it.'

'Very well,' growled Bruang from his tree. 'Now we know why the White Man clears the jungle. He gets money for it. White men love money better than food. If he gets money for it, the White Man will go on clearing the jungle. Every day there is more and more cleared land and less and less jungle, and soon there will not be enough room for all of us, that's certain. Some of us will have to swim.'

'*I* shall be waiting then,' murmured the Crocodile, snuggling his long face, with the built-in smile on it, into the warm sand.

'Well, it's a nice lookout for you four-legged beasts, that's all I can say,' chipped in the Brain-fever bird. 'As for me, I can fly, but what about you? If you swim, our friend, the Crocodile there, will eat you; and if you stay, our red-faced enemy, the White Man, will shoot you.'

'That's so,' grumbled the Bear. 'Something will have to be done.'

'Something will have to be done,' cried the other animals.

'We must think out a plan,' said the Bear slowly.

'Yes,' cried the others. 'We must think out a plan.'

'While you are thinking,' screamed the Mosquito, in his irritating treble, 'I shall go off and call on the White Man. It is long past my dinner-time,' and he flew away.

'There is only one thing to be done,' said the Stick Insect. 'The White Man must be stopped.'

'Easier said than done,' said the Flying-fox, who had hung herself upside down from a branch of the tapang tree while they were talking. Every animal looked up at her respectfully. She was supposed to live by sucking the blood of humans while she fanned them to sleep with her great leathery wings, but, as a matter of fact, the truth was that she never ate anything stronger than fruit.

'Perhaps, O wise one,' said the Stick Insect, 'you can tell us how the White Man is to be stopped?'

'There are three hundred and ninety-three ways of killing a Stick Insect,' said the Flying-fox, 'but there are only three ways of dealing with a White Man.'

'What are they?' cried all the jungle creatures in an eager chorus.

'The first way,' said the Flying-fox, 'is the way of softness, the second way is the way of cunning, and the third way is to go to law.'

'How can we get the better of the White Man by softness?' jeered the Stick Insect.

'In the same way that the Southeast wind got the better of the tree-frog,' said the Flying-fox.

'Is there a story in it?' cried all the jungle people, eagerly.

'There is,' said the Flying-fox. 'It's called

THE KING OF THE WINDS.'

'Let's hear it,' said the jungle creatures.

'Very well,' said the Flying-fox, making herself more comfortable on her tree branch. 'If you don't grunt or snuffle, I'll tell you.

14

THE KING OF THE WINDS

R. W. Coulter

THE KING OF THE WINDS

ONE fine day, said the Flying-fox, when the winds were taking a holiday and all the small white clouds were drifting about happily as if they didn't know where they were going and didn't much care, and all the fishing boats were lying becalmed on the sea, which was peacefully smiling because it was being left alone for once, and even the leaves on the trees on shore had stopped whispering to one another and were hanging down fast asleep – well, one fine day the Northwest wind, having nothing better to do, strolled over from Singapore and paid a call on the Southeast wind, who lives round about Celebes. The Northwest wind is a blusterer and given to boasting and he never misses a chance of talking about how strong he is.·

'Talking about blowing,' he said, although they weren't talking about anything of the sort. 'Yesterday, as I was passing through Kualalumpur, I blew the whiskers off a witch-doctor.'

'That was a good effort,' murmured the Southeast wind. 'Blowing whiskers off witch-doctors is good practice. When *I* want a little gentle exercise I try blowing Kodok off his cocoanut tree.'

'Fireballs and forked lightning!' growled the Northwest wind. 'Tree-frogs is poor practice. I wouldn't waste breath over them.'

'All the same,' said the Southeast wind, 'I bet you couldn't blow Kodok off his cocoanut tree.'

The Northwest wind took a short breath, which made the little clouds swim about like gold-fish, and puffed it contemptuously at the little green tree-frog. The cocoanut tree he was sitting on groaned and bent its head; but when it straightened itself Kodok was still sitting on his palm leaf smiling peacefully.

The Northwest wind now took a deep breath, which made the breakers grumble on the reef and drove all the little cloudlets helter-skelter over the skyline. The cocoanut tree screamed and bent nearly double and some of its fruit went flop, flop on the ground. But when it was over, Kodok was still in the same place and still smiling happily.

This made the Northwest wind angry. He set his teeth, went purple in the face, and sucked in all the air for a hundred miles around. All the millions of little waves woke up, put their little white caps on, and started racing madly after each other, and the fishermen buoyed their nets and ran for home. Then the Northwest wind turned on the unfortunate cocoanut tree and blew and blew and blew until all the rest of the cocoanuts flew off one after the other, and the unhappy tree bent down and down and down until it nearly touched the ground.

And when the Northwest wind had blown himself quite empty so that he could blow no more that day, there was little Kodok, swinging himself happily to and fro on his palm frond.

'Now, let me try,' purred the Southeast wind; and he pursed up his lips and blew softly and gently, so gently that the little waves took their white caps off, stopped racing about, and went tinkling on the shore like music; and the grass-blades all whispered a song and the leaves of the cocoanut tree made such a quiet lullaby as they waved gently to and fro, that presently Kodok, who was a tiny bit tired after being blown about so much by the Northwest wind, fell fast asleep. Then the Southeast wind suddenly stopped blowing, and Kodok was so surprised that he fell off. That is why they call the Southeast wind the Rajah Angin, the King of the Winds. Which shows, finished the Flying-fox, rattling her bony wings, that sometimes you can get things done just as well by being quiet and gentle as by being rough and strong.

'Humph!' said the Stick Insect when the Flying-fox had finished her story. 'I don't see the point of that. In the first place the White Man doesn't live in cocoanut trees; and, in the second place, if he did, who is going to blow him out of one?'

'Very well,' said the Flying-fox patiently, 'if we can't deal with the White Man with softness, as the Wind did to the tree-frog, then we can deal with him by cunning, as the Mouse-deer did with the Tiger.'

'Is there a story in it?' asked the Ape.

'There is,' said the Flying-fox. 'It's called

THE TIGER AND THE MOUSE-DEER.'

'Let's hear it,' cried all the jungle creatures.

'Very well,' said the Flying-fox. 'If you don't wriggle and hiss, I'll tell you.'

18

THE TIGER

and THE MOUSE-DEER

THE TIGER AND THE MOUSE-DEER

ONCE upon a time, began the Flying-fox, Mouse-deer got into a strange country. He had not gone far when the Tiger saw him. Off went the Mouse-deer and off went the Tiger after him. Up hill and down dale they went until Mouse-deer could run no farther. 'What can I do now to save myself?' thought Mouse-deer.

Just then he came to a red ants' nest.

'Good,' he said, 'I will stay by this nest.'

Up came the Tiger.

'Good-day, friend Mouse-deer,' said the Tiger, 'do you know any reason why I shouldn't eat you?'

'None whatever,' said the Mouse-deer politely, 'except that King Solomon might be angry.'

'And why should King Solomon be angry?' said the Tiger.

'Because,' said the Mouse-deer, 'I am guarding his gong.'

'Is that King Solomon's gong?' said the Tiger. 'I should very much like to strike it.'

'Strike it by all means,' said the Mouse-deer, 'but first let me go a little way away, in case King Solomon should be angry.'

So off skipped the Mouse-deer and Tiger stood off and struck at the ants' nest.

Down fell the ants in a stream and stung Tiger till he couldn't see.

Off dashed the Tiger in a rage with the ants getting a free ride all over him. Soon he saw Mouse-deer again. Up hill and down dale, over jungle and plain he chased him until Mouse-deer could run no farther. 'What shall I do this time?' thought Mouse-deer. And then he saw a clump of bamboos and went and stood by them.

'Do you know any good reason why I shouldn't eat you?' said the Tiger, coming up in a tearing fury.

'None whatever,' said the Mouse-deer respectfully, 'except that King Solomon will be angry.'

'And why will King Solomon be angry?' asked the Tiger.

'Because I am guarding his violin,' said the Mouse-deer, and he pointed to a split bamboo through which the wind was singing.

'Is that King Solomon's violin?' said the Tiger. 'I was always fond of music and I should very much like to play it.'

'Quite easy,' said the Mouse-deer. 'Put your tongue to the slit and blow for all you are worth and you'll make the loveliest music possible. But first let me go a little way off, in case King Solomon is angry.'

So off skipped Mouse-deer, and Tiger put his tongue to the slit and blew as hard as he was able. But just then the bamboo was swayed by the wind and the slit closed and bit Tiger's tongue off, and that is why Tigers have short tongues to this day.

The Tiger was furious. Off he rushed after the Mouse-deer. Up hill and down dale he chased him until the Mouse-deer could go no farther. 'What shall I do now?' he thought. Just then he saw a buffalo-wallow, and went and stood by it.

'Do you know any good reason why I shouldn't eat you?' said the Tiger fiercely.

21

'None whatever,' said the Mouse-deer, 'except that King Solomon will be angry.'

'Why will King Solomon be angry?'

'Because his rice has just finished cooking and I have been told to guard it.'

'Is that King Solomon's rice?' said the Tiger greedily. 'I should very much like to try it.'

'Very well,' said the Mouse-deer, 'but first let me go a little way off, in case King Solomon is angry.'

So off went the Mouse-deer, and the Tiger proceeded to lick up the buffalo-wallow.

'Pah!' he said, in disgust, when he got the taste of it well down his throat, 'this is not rice, this is mud!'

And he rushed off to find Mouse-deer, more furious than ever.

Up hill and down dale, over jungle and swamp he chased him until Mouse-deer could run no farther.

'What am I going to do now?' thought the Mouse-deer.

And just then he saw his old friend, Inchek Ular the Snake, coiled up under a tree having a quiet nap; so he went and stood by him.

'Now I've got you, you rascal,' said the Tiger to Mouse-deer. 'This time I don't intend to let you go! Do you know any reason why I shouldn't eat you?'

'I can only think of one for the moment," said the Mouse-deer, politely. 'King Solomon might be angry.'

'You don't catch me with that old joke this time,' said the Tiger. 'Why should King Solomon be angry?'

'Because,' said the Mouse-deer, 'he has left his best silk turban here, and I am guarding it.'

'Is that really King Solomon's turban?' said the Tiger. 'I should like above all things to wear it.'

'Put it on by all means,' said the Mouse-deer, 'but first let me get well away, in case King Solomon is angry.'

Then Mouse-deer went a long way off and looked on.

Tiger picked up King Solomon's turban and tried to put it on.

But Inchek Ular woke up, and, very annoyed at being disturbed, he wound himself round Tiger and squeezed and squeezed and squeezed until Tiger lost his breath.

'Allah Taubat!' said Tiger.

Then the snake squeezed him a little more and Tiger's bones began to crack.

'Bishmillah,' said Tiger.

Inchek Ular squeezed a little tighter.

'Allahu Akbar,' gasped the Tiger.

Inchek Ular squeezed a little tighter.

'LA ILAHA LA'LLAH,' groaned the Tiger, and then he gave up the ghost.

'Hurrah,' laughed Mouse-deer, who had been watching all the time, and on he skipped over hill and dale, through jungle and swamp, more pleased with himself than ever.

'Pooh!' said the Stick Insect when the Flying-fox had finished her second story. 'That plan is worse than the other one. Any fool knows that the White Man doesn't wear turbans.'

'Very well,' said the Flying-fox, 'if we can't get the better of the White Man by softness, as the Wind did to the tree-frog, or by cunning, as the Mouse-deer did to the Tiger, then we will have to go to Law like the Rhinoceros.'

'Is there a story in that?' asked the Hornbill.

'There is,' said the Flying-fox. 'It's called

PA BADAK'S LAWSUIT.'

'Let's hear it,' cried all the jungle creatures.

'Very well,' said the Flying-fox. 'If you don't whistle and scream, I'll tell you.'

PA BADAK'S LAWSUIT -

PA BADAK'S LAWSUIT

ONE day, said the Flying-fox, the Mouse-deer went to pay a call on Badak the Rhinoceros. Pa Badak was not at home, but his seven very little sons and his seven very little daughters were there playing in the sun.

'Where is your father, little ones?' asked the Mouse-deer.

'He has gone down to the river to bathe,' said the little rhinos. Just then the Elephant, who was nearby in the jungle, began to blow his war-trumpet. He made such a terrible noise that the birds stopped singing, the monkeys stopped chattering, and even the butterflies stopped flitting from flower to flower.

'The enemy must be coming,' said Mouse-deer, and he started to dance the war-dance. Before he knew what he was doing, the Mouse-deer had danced all over Pa Badak's children and trodden them to pieces with his sharp little feet.

'Now what am I to do?' said Mouse-deer, when he saw the little rhinos lying around dead. And off he went home, as fast as he could, to think it over.

When Pa Badak the Rhinoceros came back from his bath and found all his sons and daughters had been killed and that Mouse-deer's tracks were all around, he was very angry, and off he went to King Solomon to lay a complaint before him.

King Solomon was sitting in his court, on a golden throne, with his wives and generals around him.

'What can I do for you, Pa Badak?' said King Solomon.

'I want you to punish Mouse-deer, O King!'

'And what has Mouse-deer done to you?' asked King Solomon.

'He has danced on my children and killed them,' said Pa Badak.

King Solomon stroked his beard and told Burong Bayan, the messenger bird, to go and fetch Mouse-deer. Off flew Burong Bayan, as fast as he was able.

'Why did you kill the children of Pa Badak the Rhinoceros?' said King Solomon to the Mouse-deer, when he appeared.

'Alas, O King! the fault was not mine. I heard Elephant blowing his war-trumpet and I thought the enemy was coming, so I danced my war-dance and trod Pa Badak's children to pieces.'

King Solomon rubbed his beard and called Burong Bayan, and told him to fetch the Elephant. Off flew Burong Bayan as fast as he was able.

'Why, O Elephant!' said King Solomon, 'did you blow your trumpet and make Mouse-deer dance his war-dance so that the children of Pa Badak were killed?'

'Alas!' said the Elephant, 'it was not my fault, O King. I was walking by the river and I saw Crocodile floating down with all his armour on, and I thought the enemy was coming, and so I blew my trumpet.'

King Solomon ruffled his beard. 'Fetch the Crocodile,' he said to Burong Bayan. Off flew Burong Bayan to fetch the Crocodile, as fast as he was able.

'Why, O Crocodile!' said King Solomon, 'did you put your armour on and make Elephant blow his trumpet and Mouse-deer dance his war-dance over the children of Pa Badak the Rhinoceros, so that they all died?'

'Alas!' said the Crocodile, 'the fault was not mine. I saw Turtle swimming from the upper reaches with his shield on his back and I thought the enemy was coming, and so I put my armour on!'

King Solomon tugged at his beard and told Burong Bayan to fetch the Turtle.

'Why, thou slow-footed thing,' said King Solomon, 'did you wear your shield, so that Crocodile thought an enemy was coming and put his armour on and Elephant blew his trumpet and made Mouse-deer dance his war-dance over the children of Pa Badak the Rhinoceros?'

'It was not my fault, O King!' said the Turtle. 'I saw Nokdiak the Ant-eater running with a bundle of spears in each hand, and I thought the enemy was coming, so I picked up my shield to attack him.'

King Solomon pulled a great handful of hair out of his beard. 'Send for Sang Nokdiak,' he said.

When Sang Nokdiak came in, rustling his quills, King Solomon said, 'Why, O prickly one, do you run about my country with a bundle of spears in each hand. Do you know that only the King's men may carry arms?'

'It was not my fault, great King,' said Sang Nokdiak. 'I was going quietly down to the river to drink, and I met Pa Badak the Rhinoceros tearing along, smashing the trees down, and shouting that the enemy was after him. So I picked up my spears in both hands to throw at the enemy.'

King Solomon pulled two handfuls of hair out of his beard and turned to Pa Badak, 'Heh, Pa Badak!' he shouted, 'why did you go tearing through the jungle, smashing down the trees and shouting that an enemy was coming, when there was no enemy?'

'It was not my fault, O King!' said Pa Badak the Rhinoceros, 'I went down to the river to bathe, and when I looked into the water, there I saw an enemy, with a shining helmet on his head, just about to leap out at me. So I rushed off through the jungle to tell you, O King, that the enemy was coming!'

King Solomon was so puzzled that his beard curled up into a question mark.

'Who was this enemy?' he said.

Bantangan the Long-nosed Ape had been sitting on the branch of a tree all the time, listening to the evidence, and now he cried, 'May I speak, O King?'

'Speak on,' said the King, wearily.

'By the wisdom of Allah, O King,' said Bantangan, 'I was sitting in a tree by the side of the river when Pa Badak the Rhinoceros came down to bathe. There was no enemy, O King, with a shining helmet on his head, waiting in the water to spring on Pa Badak. Pa Badak saw only his own reflection, and, being a fool, he ran screaming through the jungle, shouting that the enemy was coming. This is the truth, O King!'

King Solomon was so angry that his beard looked like an exclamation mark.

'By the right arm of the Prophet,' he shouted, 'you are a fool, Pa Badak, and the son of a fool! You ran away from your own shadow and frightened Nokdiak the Ant-eater, and he thought the enemy was coming and took his spears in both hands, and when Turtle saw Nokdiak with his spears in both hands he put his shield on, and when the Crocodile saw the Turtle with his shield on his back he put his armour on, and when Elephant saw Crocodile with all his armour on he blew his trumpet to warn the country, and the sound of his trumpet made Mouse-

deer dance his war-dance, and so all your children got killed
The fault is not Mouse-deer's. The fault is your own. The case
is dismissed!'

'Green leaves and twigs!' cried the Stick Insect, when the
Flying-fox had finished. 'That plan is sillier than the other two.
King Solomon has power over all the birds and beasts, but
everybody knows he hasn't any power over humans.'

'Well,' said the Flying-fox humbly, 'I've done my best for
you.'

'A poor best it was too!' said the Stick Insect hastily. 'Still,
what else could one expect from a creature that is neither a bird,
a beast, nor an insect, and has wings like a crow and fur like
a rabbit, and who talks upside down?'

'Very well,' said the Flying-fox angrily, unhooking herself
from the tapang-tree. 'If you don't like my plan, think of a better
one! I'm off to the White Man's garden to see if his mangoes
are ripe yet. He can burn all your old jungle, for all I care!' and
she flapped away over the forest towards the White Man's house.

THE SECOND MEETING

THE SECOND MEETING

AT WHICH IT IS DECIDED THAT THE PYTHON SHALL KILL THE WHITE MAN

'PERHAPS,' said the Stick Insect, when the animals were all gathered together at the meeting-pool the next evening, 'perhaps, now that the Flying-fox has gone off in a huff, somebody else can oblige with a plan for dealing with the White Man.'

'You won't kill him with talk, that's certain,' growled Bruang the Bear.

'And all the time,' said the Hornbill, 'he is cutting down more and more of our jungle.'

'He's going to start burning off as soon as the rains are over,' said the Pig. 'I was under his house last evening and heard him tell Amit, the headman.'

Just then a sound like a heavy body being slowly dragged along the ground came from the dark forest behind, and every bird and animal sprang up quivering, and faced the sound, while their eyes wandered to and fro as if they would have liked to have jumped out of their sockets.

'Be seated, friends,' said the Python, lifting his small, wicked-looking head a few inches above the grass-blades. 'I have dined.'

A sigh of relief rustled through the grass and the leaves. The Python is the only creature in the jungle who does not keep the island law not to kill at the meeting-pool; and he does not keep it because he is strong enough to break it.

'I have taught manners to the White Man's dog,' he went on, coiling himself comfortably round a branch of the tapang tree, just under the bear's front door. 'I have put up with him for a long time, but he would run into the jungle and bark at my tail as if I were some sort of an earth-worm. A poor beast, the White Man's dog. All skin and bone. And he is wearing a hard leather thing round his neck with bits of brass and things on it that I'm afraid will take a lot of digesting. What is all the talk about?'

'We were just talking about you,' said the Stick Insect, who was so used to looking like what he wasn't that he could tell a lie better than anybody.

'Talking about me, were you,' said the Python, suspiciously, 'and what may you have been saying about me?'

'We were saying,' went on the Stick Insect, 'that of all the jungle creatures, the biggest, strongest, and bravest is the Python.'

'Well, what of it?' said the Python. 'I don't suppose there is any one here who will say 'No!' to that, is there?' and he swung his speckled head slowly to and fro.

There was dead silence round the meeting-pool. Bruang the Bear was the next strongest, but he was only a young bear, and he held his tongue.

'And we were saying,' went on the Stick Insect, 'what a shame it is, the way the White Man is eating up our jungle.'

'Can't say I feel very upset about that,' said the Python. 'It makes the hunting easier in the jungle that is left.'

'That's so,' said the Stick Insect. 'But what will you do when there's no jungle left at all? You will be no better off than the rest of us, and the White Man can come with a stick and kill you just as if you *were* really an earth-worm.'

'There is something in that,' said the Python.

'So,' said the Stick Insect, 'we decided that the White Man must be stopped.'

'Quite right,' said the Python. 'The White Man must be stopped.'

'And we decided,' said the Hornbill in his raucous voice, 'that you were the one to do it.'

'That,' said the Python, trying not to look upset, 'is another story. The White Man isn't as big a fool as he looks. He is not as easy to frighten as a Hornbill,' and he poked his wicked head suddenly forward right into the Hornbill's face.

The Hornbill blinked his eyes hard, but held his ground.

'Did I ever tell you,' he said, 'the story of the Squirrel and the Shellfish?'

'You never did,' cried all the birds and beasts at once, crowding round the Hornbill, who was known to be a good story-teller.

'Very well,' said the Hornbill. 'Don't scratch and rustle and I'll tell you. It's called

THE GREATEST RACE THAT EVER WAS.'

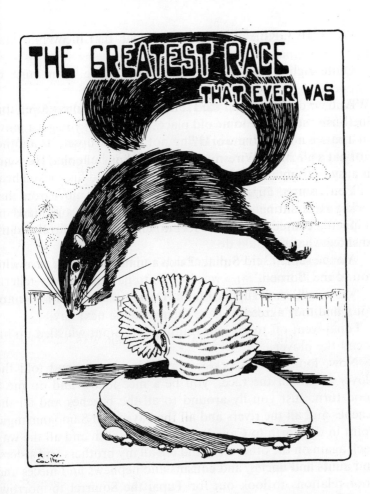

THE GREATEST RACE
THAT EVER WAS

THE GREATEST RACE THAT EVER WAS

'WELL, old Cling-fast,' said Tupai the Squirrel to Siput the Shell-fish, 'still in the same old place? Why don't you get a move on and see a bit of the world?'

'That's all right, Wirewhiskers,' said Siput. 'I could beat you in a race at any rate.'

'You!' roared Tupai. 'Why, I haven't seen you move from that rock you're sitting on since the day you were born,' and he skipped a couple of hundred feet down the beach and back just to show what he could do.

'All the same,' said Siput, 'I don't mind running a race with you round Borneo.'

'Very well,' said Tupai. 'I'll do it, just to take the lime out of you,' and they agreed to have their race the next day.

Tupai went off to go into training but Siput whistled up his friend the plover.

'Now, look here, Speckles,' he said, after he had told the plover all about the race, 'you be a nice fellow and do me a good turn. Just you fly around to all the beaches and all the reaches and all the rivers and all the bays from Sampanmangio Point in the north to Cape Puding in the south and all the way back again on the other side, and tell all my brothers and sisters, and aunts and uncles, and cousins and nephews and nieces and poor relations to look out for Tupai the Squirrel to-morrow, for I have promised to race him round Borneo. And tell them when they see him coming, to sit still on their rocks and look as like me as they can.'

So the plover flew off to all the bays and beaches, the rivers and reaches, from Sampanmangio Point in the north to Cape Puding in the south, and all the way back again on the other side, and he told all Siput's brothers and sisters and cousins and nieces and poor relations to be sitting ready on their rocks looking as much like Siput as they could.

Next day the great race started, and Tupai the Squirrel flew off from Sampanmangio Point in the north; but he didn't worry about going his fastest because he didn't think the Shellfish had a possible hope anyhow.

All the same he was out of sight before you could say 'Allah Akbar.' As for Siput, if you had looked ever so carefully at him you wouldn't have seen him move.

Nevertheless, when Tupai got to the first stopping place, there was a shellfish sitting on a rock waiting for him. Tupai was all hot and perspiry, but the shellfish was breathing gently as if he hadn't had to bustle much.

Tupai was a bit surprised, but he knew he could beat Siput if he only went fast enough; so he wound up his tail and sprang off like a streak of greased lightning; and he jumped so high that he went clean over Mount Kinabalu, which was a good jump, for Mount Kinabalu is a very high mountain, as you know.

If you had looked at the shellfish with a powerful microscope you wouldn't have been able to see him move.

All the same when Tupai landed,

plop! at the next stopping place, all hot and bothered, there was a shellfish exactly like the last, sitting on a comfortable rock, waiting for him and looking as if nothing mattered.

Off went Tupai again, without waiting to take breath. This time you could only see his head, and his body looked like a thin blue flame.

All the same, when he got to the next stopping place there was a shellfish sitting on a rock, waiting for him.

You couldn't see Tupai on the next lap; you could just hear a furry whistle, and when he landed at the next place the sand got red-hot for a moment, but there was a shellfish, just like all the other shellfish, sitting on a rock humming gently to himself.

Tupai was tired out by now, and so damp he looked as if he had had a bath. He could only just stagger to the next place, and hobble to the next place, and crawl to the place after that; and at each one there was a shellfish, exactly like all the other shellfish, ready waiting for him.

At last he tottered in to Cape Sampanmangio again.

And there was the Shellfish, exactly like all the other shellfish, waiting for him.

'Well, Siput,' said Tupai, wiping the perspiration from his forehead, 'I thought I could run, but I'm a snail alongside you.'

'And that,' said the Hornbill, when he had finished, looking pointedly at the Python, 'shows that the race isn't always to the fastest.'

'Humph!' said the Python, yawning heavily. 'If words could kill, the White Man would be dead already. Now, my friends, I've had a good dinner and I'm going torpid. You'd better get about your business.'

He coiled himself comfortably round his tree branch.

'For, as you know,' he added, as he shut his eyes, 'after a good sleep I am always specially hungry.'

THE
THIRD
MEETING

THE THIRD MEETING

AT WHICH THE PYTHON GOES TO SLEEP

'MY fatness,' squeaked the Pig, when the jungle people were gathered together at the meeting-pool the next evening. 'Things are getting worse and worse. I've just been down to the Green Swamp for my evening bathe, and it isn't there.'

'What isn't there?' asked the Stick Insect.

'The Green Swamp, of course, you idiot!' said the Pig.

'It isn't there?' cried all the other creatures. 'Swamps can't walk. Where has it gone to?'

'It has run into the sea,' said the Pig. 'It is that White Man again. I saw him looking at the swamp with his headman only yesterday. He must have done it.'

'That's right,' said the Mosquito, who had buzzed up while the Pig was talking. 'The White Man has been going to drain that swamp for a long time. I have heard him talking about it to Amit, the headman. He hates swamps.'

'Why should the White Man hate swamps?' asked the Buffalo-leech. 'What harm do they do to him? His working bullocks come every day to that swamp to get away from the flies, and while they are standing in it I feed on them. Where will I get my food now?'

'You will have to look for it somewhere else, old bloodsucker,' said the Mosquito, 'and I will have to look elsewhere for a breeding ground. The White Man says the swamp has bred leeches and mosquitoes long enough, and now it is going to grow rubber-trees.'

'Then what is to become of us?' cried the Ape.

'You can swim, of course,' murmured the Crocodile, from his bed in the warm sand.

'Either way,' went on the Mosquito, 'it won't hurt me. If the White Man goes, I feed on you, and if you go I feed on him,' and he did a tandak round the soft nose of Bruang the Bear.

'Well,' said the Mosquito, after a pause. 'There's one thing that's certain. There is only one creature strong enough to deal with the White Man, and there he lies, the lazy, overfed brute!'

Everybody looked at the Python, who was still sleeping off the meal he had made of the White Man's dog.

'Was anybody addressing me?' said the Python, opening one eye.

'We were just saying,' said the Stick Insect, telling lies as usual, 'that the noblest and bravest creature in the jungle is the Python.'

'You've said that before,' replied the Python, pretending to be annoyed, although he was secretly flattered. 'What of it?'

'The White Man is at it again,' said the Stick Insect. 'He has drained the Green Swamp and soon there'll be no more water left for us to drink. He's simply got to be dealt with, and it's your duty, as the biggest, bravest, and noblest creature in the jungle, to deal with him.'

'Yes, yes,' cried the others, 'it's the Python's plain duty to do it.'

'Bosh!' said the Python, uncoiling five or six feet of his great body and rearing it slowly in the air. 'Let's talk sense. I admit I'm the strongest and bravest, not to say noblest, creature in the jungle. I can swallow a pig, an ape, and a slow loris at one sitting. But eating White Men is a different thing. It's not my business to eat White Men. They carry things in their pockets that interfere with my digestion. Let everybody stick to his own line of business, I say. You can't make a man-eater out of a pig-eater any more than you can make a man out of a mouse, as Pa Kelau found out.'

'Is there a story in that?' asked the Stick Insect.

'Yes,' said the Python, 'and a good one, too.'

'Let's hear it,' cried all the jungle people, crowding together underneath the tapang tree.

'Don't rustle and scrape,' said the Python, 'and I'll tell you. It's called

THE GREATEST THING IN THE WORLD.'

THE GREATEST THING IN THE WORLD

THE GREATEST THING IN THE WORLD

PA KELAU and his wife, began the Python, had never had any children, although they often used to pray to Kinharingan, who lives in the sky, to send them a son. One day they were out in the rice-fields, and they were both thinking how nice it would be, now they were getting old, to have a son to plough the fields and plant the rice for them, when an eagle, which was flying overhead with a tiny mouse in its beak let it drop, and, flop! it fell, right at the feet of Pa Kelau and his wife.

'Look, wife,' said Pa Kelau, 'Kinharingan, who lives in the sky, has answered our prayer and sent us a beautiful boy.'

And they picked the mouse up and took it to their house and put a bright red coat on it, and looked after it as if it were their own son.

It was a very good son and helped them in the fields, bringing in the rice for them and never eating anything that was not given to it.

At last it grew up, and Pa Kelau one day said to his wife, 'Now, wife, the boy is a man, and it is time we found a wife for him so that he can have sons to work the fields for him when he gets old.'

So Pa Kelau went to the mouse and said to him, 'Now, my son, it is time you took a wife. Which of all the girls in the village would you like to cook your rice for you?'

'Father,' said the mouse, 'the girls of the village are a silly, giggling lot. I want none of them. If I am to marry, I will marry the greatest thing in the world!'

Pa Kelau scratched his head and went to his wife.

'Listen, wife,' he said. 'Our son says that the girls of the village are a silly, giggling lot and he will have nothing to do with them. If he is to marry he will marry the greatest thing in the world. What *is* the greatest thing in the world?'

Pa Kelau's wife thought for a day and a night, and at last she went to Pa Kelau and said, 'Surely the Sun is the greatest thing in the world.'

So Pa Kelau took some cocoanuts to drink and some rice to eat, and he went towards the sunset. He climbed the mountains and walked across the plains until he came to a little hill that was close to where the Sun went down, and there he sat down to wait until the Sun should pass.

'O, Sun!' shouted Pa Kelau, as soon as the Sun got close enough to hear him, 'my boy has grown up to be a man, and it is time he took a wife, but he will not marry any of the girls in the village for they are a silly, giggling lot. He will only marry the greatest thing in the world. Are you, O Sun, the greatest thing in the world?'

And the Sun said, 'No, I am not the greatest thing in the world. The Clouds are greater than I, for they cast their shadow over my face. Go and ask them.'

So Pa Kelau climbed the mountains and swam the rivers and walked across the plains until he came to a tall hill on which a cloud was resting.

'O, Cloud!' he whispered gently, so as not to frighten it away, 'my son has grown up to be a man and it is time he had a wife to cook his rice, but he will not marry any of the girls of the village

47

for they are a giggling, silly lot. He will only marry the greatest thing in the world. Are you the greatest thing in the world?'

But the Cloud shook its head as it drifted away from the hill. 'I am not the greatest thing in the world,' it said, 'the Wind is greater than I, for I have to go wherever it wants me to.'

So Pa Kelau climbed the mountains and swam the rivers and walked over the plains, until he saw the Wind standing on top of a high mountain blowing little clouds about with a blowpipe.

'O, Wind!' whistled Pa Kelau, through his teeth, 'my son has grown into a man and it is time he had a wife to look after the cooking-pots for him, but he will not have any of the girls of the village for they are a silly, giggling lot. He will only marry the greatest thing in the world. Are *you* the greatest thing in the world?'

The Wind stopped worrying the little clouds and looked at Pa Kelau. 'No, I am not the greatest thing in the world,' he said. 'The Mountain is greater than I, for, blow as hard as I like, I cannot make it get out of my way, and I have to go either round it or over it.'

So Pa Kelau turned to the Mountain and said, 'Then you, Mountain, must marry my son, for you are certainly the greatest thing in the world.'

But the Mountain groaned and said, 'You're quite wrong. I am not the greatest thing in the world. There is a little thing inside me which has been burrowing and burrowing until it has made a hole right through me. Whatever it is, it must be greater than I, for I can do nothing to stop it, and it has given me a terrible pain in the foot of which I'm sure I shall die.'

So Pa Kelau went to the foot of the Mountain and there he found a tiny mouse, and when he took it home and showed it to

his son, he shouted with delight, and said: 'She is the wife I have
been waiting for.' And they were married and kept house in the
hole under the mountain.

As the Python got to the end of his story his voice got drowsier
and drowsier and his head dropped lower and lower, and almost
before he had finished he had gone torpid again.

THE
FOURTH
MEETING

THE FOURTH MEETING

AT WHICH THE SLOW LORIS TALKS MAGIC

'PIG!' snorted the Stick Insect, pointing at the Python who had now been sleeping for nearly a week. 'Lazy brute! We can't expect anything from him until he has digested the White Man's dog, I can see that.'

'And in the meantime,' snapped the Fireflies, who had taken up their quarters in a screwpine by the side of the meeting-pool, 'the White Man is chopping down our favourite trees. We hate screwpines – spiky things – but soon there'll be nowhere else to go.'

They turned their tiny lamps on and off so quickly in their anger that the screwpine seemed to be lighted up by a continuous glow.

The Slow Loris, who had been sitting curled up like a woolly ball on a branch of the tapang tree, uncurled himself a little and blinked with his big round eyes at the Fireflies.

'If you would only turn off those confounded lights of yours for a moment or two,' he drawled, 'I might perhaps be able to think of a plan.'

Then he curled himself up again and seemed to go to sleep.

'Sh-sh,' whispered the Stick Insect. 'Don't disturb him. He's thinking out a plan.'

'I'll bet,' squattered the Buffalo-leech, 'it's a magic.'

'Sh-sh!' whispered the Stick Insect. 'Of course it's a magic.'

Everybody looked respectfully at the Slow Loris.

'They say it can live for ever,' squeaked Babi the Pig, after a while.

'You know nothing about it,' whispered the Stick Insect. 'It doesn't live for ever, but it's very hard to kill. The Dyaks can't kill it with their blowpipe darts any more than the White Man can with his double-barrelled gun. It can't be killed with fire, water, iron, or wood, but it can be killed with brass, and if the White Man only used brass instead of lead bullets he could kill it; but he doesn't know. When the humans find a dead Loris they make strong medicine out of its bones. If you lay the bone of its right leg on the ground when you chop down a tree, the tree will fall in the right direction. If you rub its tears on your eyes you can see ghosts, and its blood smeared on the mouth of the cooking-pot makes the rice last for ever. If a human wants to steal his next-door neighbour's goods, he rubs the Slow Loris' fur on the legs of the house and everybody inside the house will fall asleep. If – sh-sh, he's waking up!'

A little shiver ran over the Slow Loris' body and his large round eyes gradually appeared, like two yellow moons rising together.

'Well,' cried all the jungle people eagerly, 'have you thought out a plan?'

'Did I ever,' drawled the Slow Loris in his weary tones, – 'did I ever tell you that story about the Jellyfish?'

'You never did,' they all cried.

'It's only a short story,' said the Slow Loris thoughtfully, 'but it's a very good story. It's called

THE JELLYFISH THAT WOULDN'T.'

'Let's hear it,' cried all the jungle people.

'Very well,' said the Slow Loris. 'If you don't hiss and bristle, I'll tell it to you.'

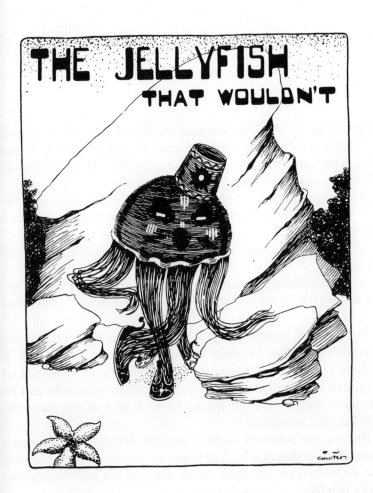

THE JELLYFISH THAT WOULDN'T

THERE was a Jellyfish once, said the Slow Loris – a very young Jellyfish – who wouldn't believe what his parents told him, but always thought he knew better. 'The safest place for a very young jellyfish,' said his mother, 'is in the sea.'

But he wouldn't believe her. 'I'm sick of floating around in the sea,' he said to himself one day; 'it wouldn't be bad fun to have a run on shore.'

So he put on his best hat and his two best pairs of slippers, and off he went.

At first he thought it was fine on shore – 'I wouldn't be in the sea for anything,' he said. Just then the Sun saw him and smiled on him.

The Jellyfish began to feel all funny about the legs, and the perspiration began to creep under his best hat and he felt it wouldn't be a bad thing to sit down and mop his face, but he had forgotten his handkerchief. He had a frightful headache and he felt like crying – and he would have, if he had not been the Jellyfish that wouldn't.

But the sun went on smiling, and the Jellyfish felt his knees knocking together and his legs began to run into his best slippers, and he wished he was back in the sea with his parents and the other jellyfish.

But it was too late, because his legs were bending all ways at once, and when he tried to walk he just went round and round. Then he began to sag in the middle and his best hat slipped off,

nd his cheeks melted into his mouth, and then he felt so tired he
imply had to sit down.

Then he fainted.

The sun went on smiling, and when the Prawn, who had been
ent by his mother to bring the Jellyfish home, came to the place
vhere he had been standing, all he could find were his best hat
and his best slippers and a damp spot on the sand.

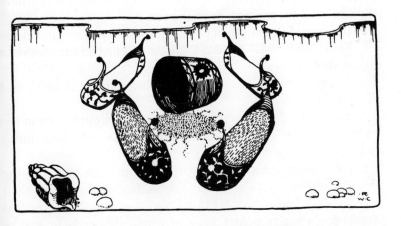

'What does that show?' asked the Stick Insect.

'It shows,' said the Slow Loris, stretching himself sleepily,
'you should never disobey your parents on a sunny day.'

'But what has that got to do with your plan for killing the
White Man?' asked the Hornbill.

'Nothing whatever,' said the Slow Loris, getting up and slowly
walking off into the forest along the upper branches of the trees.

The jungle people silently watched him fade into the night,
until all they could see of him were his two great eyes looking

back at them occasionally, like two moons wandering through the trees. Just before they vanished a low chuckle came from the forest and one of the eyes slowly disappeared.

'Do you know what he is doing?' said the Stick Insect. 'He's winking at us! Good old Slow Loris, he's thought out a big magic. That's why he wouldn't tell us about it!'

THE
FIFTH
MEETING

THE FIFTH MEETING

AT WHICH THE SLOW LORIS GOES TO SLEEP AND THE MOSQUITO TELLS A STORY

THE APE came swinging through the trees the next evening, sat down by the side of the meeting-pool and started grinning at his own reflection in the water.

'What are you grimacing at?' said the Stick Insect angrily.

'I've played a perfectly priceless trick on the White Man,' said the Ape. 'He didn't come down to the plantation to-day, so all the coolies went off to sleep in the shade. I pulled up the young rubber-trees they had planted and replanted them in the jungle.'

'And the White Man didn't come down?' asked the Stick Insect.

'No animal's seen him all day,' said the Ape.

'There you are,' cried the Stick Insect excitedly. 'I told you so!'

'Told us what?' grunted Bruang the Bear from his hole in the tapang tree.

'The Slow Loris has done it,' shouted the Stick Insect. 'Good old Slow Loris! He has made a magic and frightened the White Man away.'

'Not much, he hasn't,' squeaked Babi the Pig, who had come along the beach at that moment. 'The White Man hasn't been frightened away. I have just been under his house looking for scraps and I saw him as plainly as I see you.'

'H'm!' said the Stick Insect, looking rather foolish, 'Perhaps you can tell us what he was doing, since you're so clever.'

'He was lying in bed,' said the Pig, 'and he seemed to be sick. He was shaking so much that the house rocked.'

'Better and better,' cried the Stick Insect, getting excited again. 'It is the Slow Loris' magic has done it! He has bewitched the White Man and made him sick and in a few days he will be dead,' and he began to wave his arms and legs in pairs in the air one after the other.

'Fiddlesticks!' growled the Bear. 'I don't believe it.'

'Who cares what you believe,' shrieked the Stick Insect, working himself up into a passion. '*You're* only a child! Anyhow, here comes the Slow Loris himself. *He'll* tell us.'

Away in the depths of the forest the animals saw two yellow lights. They got bigger and bigger until they looked like twin moons floating along together under the trees; and presently the Slow Loris crawled out of the dark and curled wearily up on his branch on the tapang tree.

'Hail, great magician,' cried the Stick Insect, importantly, holding up one pair of arms and one pair of legs in an attitude of adoration. 'We have heard of your mighty deeds, how you have defeated the White Man and stricken him with a deadly sickness, so that in a few days he will die of it. Hail once more, great magician. All who creep, swim, fly, and shuffle greet you. We are your slaves for ever!' and he stood up on a twig and made the Slow Loris a sweeping bow.

The Slow Loris turned both his great eyes on the Stick Insect and smiled, but said nothing.

'Tell us, O mighty magic-maker,' went on the Stick Insect, 'how you did the magic which made the White Man sick.'

'Yes,' cried Rawa the big white pigeon, 'tell us, O mighty one!'

The Slow Loris lowered one of his eyelids, so that only one of his eyes gleamed like a yellow moon in his face.

'Have you ever heard the story of Lazy Tok?' he drawled.

'We never have,' cried all the animals at once.

'Very well,' said the Slow Loris, 'if you're very quiet and don't scuffle and stamp I'll tell you.'

LAZY TAK

LAZY TOK

TOK was born lazy, began the Slow Loris, clearing his throat. When she was a baby everybody said what a good baby she was because she never cried, but really she was too lazy to cry. It was too much trouble. The older she grew the lazier she became, until she got so lazy that she was too tired to go and look for food for herself. One day she was sitting by the side of the river, too lazy to wonder where her next meal was coming from, when a Nipah tree on the other side of the river spoke to her.

'Good evening, Tok,' he said. 'Would you like to know how to get your meals without having to work for them?'

Tok was too lazy to answer, but she nodded her head.

'Well, come over here and I'll tell you,' said the Nipah tree.

'Oh, I'm much too weary to come over there. Couldn't you come over here?' yawned Tok.

'Very well,' said the Nipah tree, and he bent over the river.

'Just tear off one of my branches,' he said.

'Oh, what a nuisance,' said Tok. 'Couldn't you shake one down yourself?'

So the Nipah tree shook himself and down dropped one of his branches at Tok's feet.

'Good evening, Tok,' said the Nipah branch. 'Would you like to be able to get your meals without having to work for them?'

Tok was too lazy to answer, but she nodded her head.

'Well,' said the Nipah branch, 'all you've got to do is to make a basket out of me.'

'Good gracious,' said Tok. 'What a bother. Couldn't you make yourself into a basket without my help?'

'Oh, very well,' said the Nipah branch, and he made himself into a nice, neat, wide, fat basket.

'Good evening, Tok,' said the Basket. 'Would you like to be

64

ble to get your meals without having to work for them?'

Tok was too lazy to answer, but she nodded her head.

'Then pick me up,' said the Basket, 'and carry me to the edge of the road and leave me there.'

'Good gracious me,' said Tok, 'do you think I'm a slave? Couldn't you pick yourself up and go without bothering me?'

'Oh, very well,' said the Basket, and he picked himself up and went off and laid himself down by the side of the road.

He hadn't been waiting there long before a fat Chinaman came along.

'Shen mao tung shi!' said the Chinaman. 'Here's a fine basket that somebody has dropped. It will just do for me to carry my goods home from market in.'

So he picked up the Basket and went off to market with it: He soon had it full of rice, potatoes, pumeloes, durians, dried shrimps, and other things too numerous to mention, and when it was full up he started off home with it.

After a while he felt hot and tired, so he put the Basket down under a tree and went off to sleep. As soon as the Basket saw that the Chinaman was fast asleep up it jumped, and ran away back to Lazy Tok.

'Here I am,' said the Basket. 'Here I am, full to the brim. You have only to empty me out, and you will have enough food to last you for a week.'

'Dear, oh, dear!' said Lazy Tok. 'What a bother. Couldn't you empty yourself out?'

'Oh, very well,' said the Basket, cheerfully, and he emptied himself into Tok's lap.

Next week, when Tok had eaten all the food, the Basket went off again and lay down on the grass by the side of the road. This time a Booloodoopy came along, and when he saw the Basket he thought it would be fine to carry his goods home from market; so he picked it up and took it off to the market. When it was full of pineapples and pumeloes and all sorts of nice things too numerous to mention, he started off home with it, but he hadn't gone far before he felt tired and hot and sat down on the side of the road to have a nap. As soon as he had fallen asleep up jumped the Basket and ran home to Lazy Tok.

So every week the Basket got itself carried to the market and came back full of fruit and rice and all sorts of other nice things too numerous to mention; and Lazy Tok sat on the river bank and ate and ate and ate and got fatter and fatter and lazier and lazier, until she became so fat and so lazy that she simply couldn't feed herself.

'Here we are waiting to be eaten,' said the fruit and the shrimps and the other nice things one day.

'Oh, bother,' said Lazy Tok. 'Couldn't you feed me yourself, without giving me so much trouble?'

'We'll try,' said the fruit and the shrimps and the other nice things; so after that they used to drop into her mouth without giving her any unnecessary trouble.

So Lazy Tok grew fatter and FATTER and FATTER, and lazier and LAZIER and LAZIER; until one day the Basket went off to lie down by the side of the road, just when the fat Chinaman who had picked it up the first time came along.

'Twee!' he said angrily. 'There you are, you thieving scoundrel!' and he picked up the Basket and took it to the market to show all his friends what had been robbing them. All his friends came round and looked at the Basket and cried, 'That is the rascal that has been robbing us!'

So they took the Basket and filled it full of soldier ants, lizards, hot-footed scorpions, bees, wasps, leeches, and all sorts of other creeping, prickling, biting, stinging, tickling, and itchy things far too unpleasant to mention; after which they let the Basket go.

Off ran the Basket with his load of bugs and beetles and centipedes and gnats and ran straight home to Lazy Tok.

'What have you got for me to-day?' asked Lazy Tok.

'You'd better get up and look,' said the Basket.

'Oh, dear me, no!' said Tok. 'I'm so tired, and I feel I couldn't stir a finger. Just empty yourself into my lap.'

So the Basket emptied the ants and beetles, and other things too horrible to mention, into Lazy Tok's lap.

Lazy Tok got up and ran and ran and ran, as she had never run in her life before. But the ants, beetles, and scorpions ran after her, and the leeches and lizards crawled after her, and the wasps and bees flew after her; and they stung her and bit her and pricked her; and the harder she ran the harder they bit her. As far as I know she may be running still, and she is thinner than ever.

'It was a good story,' said the Stick Insect, when the Slow Loris had finished, 'but what has it got to do with the magic you did to make the White Man sick?'

67

'Nothing whatever,' said the Slow Loris, curling himself up into a ball and going straight off to sleep.

'There you are,' cried the Stick Insect, triumphantly, 'I told you so!'

'What did you tell us?' growled Bruang the Bear.

'That the Slow Loris was a great magician,' cried the Stick Insect. 'Great magicians never tell their secrets to fools like you. Three cheers for the Slow Loris,' and the Stick Insect looked more important than ever as he led the cheering.

Just then the Mosquito came humming through the trees.

'What are you all shouting about?' he buzzed. 'I could hear you half-way across the island.'

'Green leaves and twigs, haven't you heard?' cried the Stick Insect. 'We were just giving three cheers for the Slow Loris because he has done a big magic and made the White Man sick.'

'Rubbidge!' buzzed the Mosquito. 'The White Man is as well as you are. I have just been sitting on his shoulder, so I ought to know,' and he did a couple of somersaults and settled down on the Slow Loris' back.

'As for your great magician, he couldn't bewitch a blowfly,' he went on. 'The White Man has a magic which is stronger than the Slow Loris' magic and he keeps it in a bottle.'

'What sort of a magic is it?' asked the Ape.

'I don't know,' said the Mosquito, 'but it's marked Quinine Bisulphate on the lable. It's the strongest magic in the world. It's stronger even than my magic.'

'Your magic,' shouted the Stick Insect. 'That's a good one. Whoever heard of a little wisp like you having a magic.'

'That's all you know about it,' buzzed the Mosquito. 'You know what the Mouse-deer did to the Elephant?'

The jungle people are always ready to listen to a story even if they have heard it a dozen times before.

'No, we don't,' they all shouted.

'Well, if you don't grunt or rumble I'll tell it to you,' said the Mosquito. 'It's called

THE FEAST OF THE DURIANS.'

THE FEAST OF THE DURIANS

THE FEAST OF THE DURIANS

ONE day as the Mouse-deer and the Elephant were having their morning bath together, the Mouse-deer, as usual, started boasting. The Elephant, being a patient beast, just squirted water over himself and said nothing.

'Fine chap you call yourself,' said the Mouse-deer, 'I daresay, but I can run faster, jump higher, and smell farther than you can any day.'

The Elephant went on with his shower-bath and said nothing.

'I can do all that,' went on the Mouse-deer, 'and what's more, I can hide myself in a cocoanut shell, which is more than you can do.'

The Elephant ran a stream of water down his spine and said nothing.

'And look here,' shouted the Mouse-deer, getting annoyed, 'you may be able to drink a bathful of dirty water, but I bet you I can eat more durians than you can, big as you are.'

The Elephant stopped his shower-bath and looked at the Mouse-deer.

'Oh,' said he, coiling up his trunk, 'you can eat more durians than I can, you think? Well, I don't mind taking you on at that.'

So they agreed to come back to the river at daylight the next morning and see who could eat the most durians. Now the Mouse-deer was a bit worried. He hadn't expected the Elephant to take him up so quickly. He had just been carried away with his own importance and hadn't the least notion how he was going to eat more durians than the Elephant. For one thing he wasn't strong enough to pull the skin off a durian. Their nasty sharp spikes stuck into him and their smell always made him sick. So he went off slowly, thinking. He hadn't gone more than six blowpipe lengths before he got an idea. He paid a call on the Orang Utan, whom he found, as usual, at home at the top of a durian tree.

'Good day, friend Orang,' said the Mouse-deer.

'Good day, brother Mouse-deer,' said the Orang.

'It'll be a fine day if it doesn't rain, friend Orang.'

'It will that, brother Mouse-deer.'

With that the Mouse-deer picked up a stone and threw it at the Orang. Smack! It hit the Orang on the head.

That made him very angry.

He picked a durian and threw it at the Mouse-deer, but the Mouse-deer skipped to one side and laughed at him.

'Bad shot, friend Orang,' said the Mouse-deer. 'Try again!' And he threw another stone and hit the Orang in the stomach.

So they went on, the Mouse-deer throwing stones at the Orang and the Orang throwing durians at the Mouse-deer until there was a pile of durians on the ground and no durians at all on the tree.

'Thanks, friend Orang,' said the Mouse-deer, 'that'll do nicely. I hope you'll like the taste of the stones I've given you,' and he skipped away.

After a while he heard 'Hok-hok' up in a tall tree, and there was his friend, the Rhinoceros Hornbill.

'Good evening, Mr Hornbill,' said the Mouse-deer. 'It's been a fine day.'

'Good evening, brother Mouse-deer,' said the Hornbill. 'It's been a very fine day.'

'Do you like durians?' asked the Mouse-deer.

'Do I like durians?' said the Hornbill. 'Do I like myself?'

'Well, go down to the river right away, and you'll find plenty,' said the Mouse-deer.

A little farther on the Mouse-deer met the Biawak.

'Good day, Sang Biawak,' he said. 'It's been a fine day.'

'It's been a fine day, friend Mouse-deer,' said the Biawak.

'Do you like durians?' asked the Mouse-deer.

'Do I like myself?' said the Biawak, licking his lips with his long tongue.

'Good,' said the Mouse-deer. 'Just run along to the river and you'll find plenty.'

The Mouse-deer went on a little, till he met the Crocodile. 'What news, friend Crocodile?' said the Mouse-deer.

'Good news, friend Mouse-deer,' said the Crocodile.

'It's been a fine day,' said the Mouse-deer.

'By the mercy of Allah,' said the Crocodile, 'it's been a nice day.'

'Do you like durians?' said the Mouse-deer.

'Allah be praised,' said the Crocodile, 'I like nothing better.'

'Then get along to the river and you will find plenty,' said the Mouse-deer.

And so the Mouse-deer went on and met the Pelican, and the Cassowary, and the Maleo, and the Monitor Lizard, and the Burong Kuntal, and the Junai, and the Opossum; and he told them all where to find the durians. Then he trotted off home, well pleased with himself, to wait till the morning.

The next morning, early, before the sun was up, the Mouse-deer went along to the river, and just as he had expected, all the birds and animals he had spoken to, and all their brothers and sisters, their aunts and their cousins, and their nephews and poor relations, had been along to eat the durians, and there were piles and piles of durian skins lying about, enough to fill a head house. So he scrapes all the skins together and makes one big pile.

Presently the Mouse-deer heard the Elephant coming, flip, flop, through the jungle, so up he climbs to the top of the pile of durian skins and taking a piece in his hand, pretends to chew it.

'What news, friend Mouse-deer?' says the Elephant. 'I fancy t'll be a nice day.'

'Good news, Mr Elephant,' says the Mouse-deer. 'By the blessing of Allah it will be a nice day.'

'I hope,' says the Elephant, 'I'm not late.'

'Well, you are a little,' says the Mouse-deer, 'but we can start as soon as you're ready.'

'What's all this pile of skins?' says the Elephant.

'Well,' says the Mouse-deer, 'it's this way. As you were late and I was feeling a bit peckish, I just had a small snack to go on with.'

The Elephant's eyes nearly dropped out of his head.

'In that case,' he says, 'we'd better call it off, because your appetite must be quite spoiled.'

'Not at all,' said the Mouse-deer, 'as a matter of fact I feel hungrier than ever.'

'Then you beat me,' says the Elephant; 'if you eat a small hill by way of a snack, you must want a range of mountains for a meal.' And he went off home, smashing up a Dyak headhouse on the way to relieve his feelings.

'So you see,' said the Mosquito, when he had finished his story, 'bigness doesn't always count.'

'I quite agree with you,' said the Stick Insect, a little more respectfully. 'But would you be good enough to tell us what magic you used to make the White Man sick?'

'Just bit him,' said the Mosquito.

75

'Hok-hok,' screamed the Hornbill. 'That's a bit too thick You don't expect us to believe that, do you?'

'Perhaps,' said the Mosquito, buzzing angrily, 'perhaps you'v never heard what the White Man calls me?'

'No,' said the Stick Insect, with mock politeness, 'we certainl haven't.'

'He calls me,' said the Mosquito, 'he calls me The Dreade Anopheles.'

'What's that mean?' asked the Ape.

'I don't know, exactly,' said the Mosquito. 'All I do know i that he thinks I'm a holy terror. He is a great hunter, is th White Man. He shoots elephants and tigers. He isn't a bi frightened of Bruang – or of the Python, for that matter. But he' frightened of me. He'd sooner be bitten by the cobra da capell than by me.'

'How do you know all this?' asked the Stick Insect, sus piciously.

'Well,' said the Mosquito, 'when he hears my hum he says "there's the dreaded Anopheles!" and he swallows some of th magic he keeps in a bottle and creeps inside his mosquito-net.'

'We are very pleased to hear all this,' said the Stick Insect more politely than he had ever spoken to any fellow-insect before. 'I what you say is true we hail you as our great deliverer.'

'Great driveller!' snapped the Mosquito rudely, jumping up and spinning round and round in the air. 'You needn't get excited. It takes years and years to kill a White Man with my magic, and when I do, thank heaven, another White Man always comes in his place. Good-bye! I'm going to frighten the White Man under his mosquito-net again,' and he sailed off over the trees in the direction of the White Man's house.

76

THE
SIXTH
MEETING

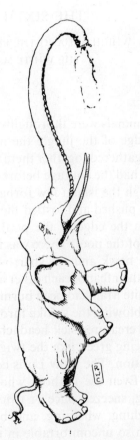

THE SIXTH MEETING

AT WHICH BRUANG THE BEAR CONFESSES TO BEING THE WHITE MAN'S FRIEND

THE animals were thoroughly miserable down at the pool on the edge of the jungle the next evening. There were more creatures gathered together there than ever before. Many of them had never had the courage before to come where the others were, even though the island law forbade killing at the meeting-pool. Now they pushed and jostled their neighbours to get as close as possible to the edge of the pool. Some of them even stood in the water of the pool. There was the little bamboo rat crouching beside the hawk and the sparrow beside the iguana. They had forgotten their fear of each other in their terror of the White Man.

The White Man had been burning the fallen jungle all day, and the wind, blowing the smoke through the green forest, had given the jungle creatures sick headaches. The Stick Insect's nose instead of being green like the twig he was standing on, was pink with irritation. The Slow Loris could hardly see out of his eyes for tears. Even the Python, who was still digesting the White Man's dog, sneezed once or twice in his sleep. All the animals were coughing, wheezing, and blowing their noses. They had never been so uncomfortable in their lives. Only the Crocodile didn't seem to worry. He lay on the sand warming his stomach and smiling his built-in smile which never seemed to match his nasty rows of teeth.

'This is frightful,' wept the Pig, as a fresh puff of smoke blew across the meeting-pool.

'It simply can't go on,' snuffled Bruang, who was having as bad a time as anybody on account of the tenderness of his nose.

'Well,' said the Stick Insect, turning to the bear, 'why don't *you* do something? After that lazy brute, the Python, you're the strongest creature in the jungle. It's your duty to put a stop to it,' and he sneezed seventeen times without stopping, so that his nose went pinker than ever.

'Of course,' cried all the animals. 'It's the Bear's plain duty.'

'No, thanks,' said Bruang. 'If I was a full-grown bear it might be another matter, but I'm only a young one.'

'Listen to him,' said the Pig. 'Any one would think he'd never heard about the baby monkey and the elephants!'

'Is there a story in it?' cried all the animals eagerly, forgetting their pains and fears.

'Of course there is,' said the Pig.

'Then let's hear it,' cried everybody, crowding round him.

'Very well, if you don't ruffle and scrape I'll tell you,' said the Pig. 'It's called

THE MESSENGER OF THE MOON.'

THE MESSENGER
OF THE MOON

THE MESSENGER OF THE MOON

THERE was a drought in the Elephant country, began the Pi
There hadn't been a drop of rain for weeks. All the pools and th
lakes had dried up, and instead of a beautiful broad river to bath
in, all the elephants had was a little muddy trickle of water whic
was hardly enough to give them each a drink, not to speak of
bath. So the King of the Elephants sent a messenger out to see i
in another part of the country, there was any water to be foun
The messenger travelled for many days over the hills and throug
the jungle, and everywhere he found the lakes had all dried u
and the pools were all gone and the rivers were just little mudd
trickles of water. But at last, after many days of travellin
he came to a river where the grass was still green and the wate
was lovely and deep, and after drinking a little and giving himse
a shower-bath, hurried back to the King to tell him the goo
news. As soon as the King of the Elephants heard it, he told h
people all to follow him, and set off to find the wonderful rive

Now the river belonged to a tribe of monkeys, and when som
of the monkey people saw the elephants coming they went to thei
King and said, 'What shall we do, O King? The elephant peopl
are coming, like mountains walking, to take our river from us

The Monkey King called all his people together and asked th
oldest and wisest monkeys to tell him how he could stop th
elephant people coming and drinking up their river. Some sai
one thing and some said another, but none of them could tell hin
how the elephant people could be stopped from drinking up thei
river. At last a little baby monkey jumped up and said, 'I will sto

nese elephants from stealing our beautiful river and drinking it
ll up.' The monkey people all laughed at him and cried, 'How

vill you, a little whipper-snapper that a baby elephant could
crush under one foot, stop a whole tribe of elephants?'

'That is my business,' said the little monkey, 'just you wait and
see!'

So the little monkey went off and climbed a tree that leaned
over the river and waited for the elephants. Soon they came
along, hundreds of big old-man elephants and hundreds of big

old-mother elephants and lots of little baby elephants who coul
have crushed the little monkey with one foot; and the groun
shook under their tread, and the trees bent as if a strong win
were blowing, and all the leaves trembled. The little monkey di
not tremble. He said in his squeaky voice, 'Stop! Stop, all yo
elephant people! If you go another step farther you will b
sorry for it!'

The elephants all stopped and looked up, and when they saw
little monkey on a tree branch they laughed, and their King saic
'Who are you, small hairy thing, that tells the elephant tribe t
stop? Come down from your tree and our baby elephants wi
trample you to death!'

'I am the messenger of the Moon, and the Moon owns all thi
river,' said the little monkey. 'There she is, bathing in it at thi
moment, and if you dare disturb her she will be very angry, an
will certainly eat you all up!'

The elephants all looked at the river, and there, sure enough
was the Moon bathing in it.

So they all gathered at the bank of the river and talked abou
what was the best thing to do; some said one thing and some saic
another, but before they had made up their minds, a little baby
elephant, trying to push its way to the front so that it could hea
what its elders were talking about, fell flop! into the river. A
once the Moon stopped bathing and began to rush up and dowr
and round and round, as if she was terribly angry. The Elephan
King, thinking he was going to be eaten, gave a wild scream anc
rushed away; and all the elephant tribe, the big old-man elephants and the big old-mother elephants and all the little baby
elephants, rushed after him, falling over each other in their hurry.
The baby elephant who had fallen into the river pulled himself
out as fast as he was able, and ran too. But after a while, noticing

hat the Moon wasn't following him, he stopped, and as he was very thirsty, he came tiptoeing back to the river, and there was the Moon, bathing herself quietly again. So he gently put his trunk into the water and took a little sip; and then, as the Moon did not seem to mind, he took a long gulp, and then he slipped down the bank, splosh! into the water and gave himself a shower-bath.

When he had had enough, very well pleased with himself, he ran after the rest of the elephants to tell them that it was alright and that there was nothing to be afraid of. He had not gone very far when he met his mother, looking very pale and anxious. 'You young brat,' she said, 'wherever have you been? I was quite sure the Moon had caught and eaten you.'

'Caught and eaten me?' said the baby elephant, 'not much, mother dear. Why, that Moon you were all so afraid of was only a reflection. I've just had a lovely shower-bath in her river, and if you all come back you can have one, too!'

'Hold your tongue, you cheeky little brat, and come along,' said the mother elephant, cuffing him over the head with her trunk, and hurrying to catch up with the rest.

So the elephant tribe went back to their own country and the monkey tribe kept their beautiful river.

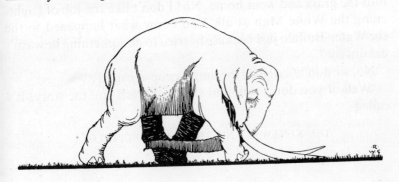

'Which shows,' said the Pig, when he had finished his story, 'that children are sometimes very much cleverer than their parents.'

'Hear, hear,' said a young lizard, but was promptly bitten by its mother.

'All the same,' said Bruang the Bear, 'I don't care for the job of frightening the White Man at all. He's not so easy to frighten either. I'll tell you what happened down at the coolie-lines one day. A Bandjermasin man got a touch of the sun and went amokking through the village slashing at everybody with his kris. When the White Man heard the noise he picked up his little malacca cane and walked out of his house, down the path towards the village. The Bandjermasin man came tearing up the path with his kris and the White Man came walking down with his little cane, but the nearer the Bandjermasin man got to the White Man the slower he ran. And at last the Bandjermasin man stopped and stood still in the middle of the path, looking as silly as a honey-bird fascinated by a snake. What do you think the White Man did? He just walked up to the Banjermasin man and tapped him on the arm and said, 'Jangan bodoh,' which means, don't be foolish, and the Bandjermasin man threw his kris into the grass and went home. No! I don't like the job of frightening the White Man at all. You know what happened to the the Water-Buffalo just because he tried to do something he wasn't cut out for?'

'No, we don't,' cried all the jungle people, eagerly.

'Well, if you don't sniff and shuffle, I'll tell you the story. It's called

THE KENAWAI AND THE WATER-BUFFALO.'

THE KENAWAI·
AND THE WATER·BUFFALO

THE KENAWAI AND THE WATER-BUFFALO

'UGH,' said Kenawai, the rice-bird, perching himself cheekily o[n] the Water-Buffalo's horns. 'I'm so thirsty I could easily drin[k] this rice-swamp dry.'

'That's all right as a figure of speech.' said the Water-Buffalo 'but, as a matter of solemn fact, you couldn't drink the milk of [a] young cocoanut.'

Just then Kenawai noticed the owner of the rice-field they were in coming to let the water out.

'As a matter of solemn fact,' said Kenawai, 'I could drink this rice-field dry, and if you agree to drink all the water in that rice-field over there. I'll drink all the water in this one.'

'All right.' said the Water-Buffalo, being quite sure the Kenawai would never be able to do it. So down hopped Kenawai and dipped his beak into the water and began to suck.

It wasn't long before all the water had run out and the swamp was dry.

'Well, well,' said the Water-Buffalo, 'you certainly did have a thirst, but if a whipper-snapper like you can drain a rice-swamp, I'm sure a big fellow like me should be able to.'

So they both went to the other rice-field, and the Water-Buffalo dipped his nose into the water and began to suck. Just then the owner came along and began to let the water in.

The Water-Buffalo sucked and sucked and sucked, but the more he sucked the higher the water rose. So he sucked and sucked and sucked and sucked, until he got blue in the face and the more he sucked the bigger he got; and he got bigger and bigger and bigger and bigger, and bigger even than that; and his skin got tighter and tighter and tighter, and tighter even than that.

But still the water rose.

So he took a deep breath and started again; but he had gone too far this time, and all of a sudden there was A BANG! and all the nuts blew off the cocoanut trees and all the bolts blew off the houses; and when Kenawai recovered from the shock and looked for the Water-Buffalo, there was nothing left of him except his horns.

After that Kenawai was called Raja Kerbau, the King of the Water-Buffaloes; and that is why you always see him like a king riding on the buffaloes' horns.

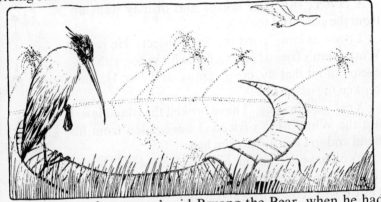

'Which just shows you,' said Bruang the Bear, when he had finished, 'that it's a great mistake to bite off more than you can chew.'

'Pooh!' said the Stick Insect. 'I know what it is. You're afraid!'

'That's it,' cried the Hornbill. 'He's afraid!'

'He's afraid of the White Man,' cried all the others in a chorus. 'The coward!'

'You can call me a coward if you like,' growled Bruang. 'but there's one thing you know as well as I do. If Penglima Alam the Tiger came walking down that path' (all the four-legged creatures looked hastily over their shoulders and their fur stood up on end at the very thought, although they knew perfectly well that there were no tigers on the island) 'if Penglima Alam came walking down that path there's only one of us who wouldn't get out of his way – and you know who that is. No, it is not I who am afraid of the White Man.'

'Then why don't you go off and kill him?' jeered the Stick Insect.

'Because,' said Bruang the Bear, 'I am the White Man's friend.'

A perfect shriek of horror and dismay went up from the grass and the leaves.

'Listen to him,' cried the Stick Insect. 'He is the White Man's friend! He has made his peace with the enemy of all that fly, creep, crawl, and run. He has broken the island law!'

'Yes,' said Bruang, 'I have broken the island law. I am the White Man's friend. I have eaten from his hand and so I will not do him harm.'

'You have eaten from his hand!' cried the Hornbill. 'How can a wild animal eat from the hand of a man? Only horses, cows, and cats do that.'

'When I was a cub,' said the Bear, 'our friend down there, the Python, killed my mother. He would have killed me, too, if the White Man hadn't come along and picked me up and taken me to his house. The White Man took me and fed me from a bottle until I was old enough to eat strong food; then he searched the forest every day for honey, nuts, and fruit. I lived in the house and played with the White Man's child. They neither beat me nor chained me up. I lived with them for the space of a wet and a dry monsoon; and then I walked back into the jungle again, because my teeth had grown long and my claws sharp, and I needed meat. That is why I will not kill the White Man.'

THE
SEVENTH
MEETING

THE SEVENTH MEETING

AT WHICH THE PYTHON WAKES UP

'B-Z-Z,' said the Mosquito, rushing up to the meeting-pool the next evening in a terrific hurry. 'Have you heard the news?'

'What news?' cried all the jungle people.

'Phew!' gasped the Mosquito. 'I am hot. I've flown all the way from the White Man's house without a stop.'

'Don't worry about how hot you are,' said the Stick Insect. 'Let's hear your news.'

'It's about the White Man's child,' said the Mosquito.

'What's the matter with the White Man's child?' asked the Stick Insect.

'It's lost and can't be found,' said the Mosquito. 'Its mother is crying up and down the beach and its father is running shouting up and down the hills, looking for it. I met the Iguana, and he says he saw it down by the lagoon an hour ago.'

'What's that you say?' said the Crocodile, getting ready to slide into the water. 'Down by the lagoon, eh? I must look into this,' and he sank under the surface without leaving a ripple behind him, and slipped away like a grey shadow in the direction of the lagoon.

Just then the little Bamboo-rat came scampering silently through the trees.

'Hi, you people!' he shouted. 'I've just seen the queerest thing in the animal world. I've seen nothing quite like it in the jungle

efore. At first I thought it was a monkey, but it's got no tail, as
ar as I could see. It's got hair as yellow as a ripe banana, eyes as
lue as the sky, and a skin as pink as the fruit of the jambu. It's
alking on its hind legs with its thumb in its mouth and I don't
hink it can see in the dark. Whose cub is it, can you tell me that?'

'It must be the White Man's child,' said the Stick Insect.
leefully. 'Which way was it going?'

'It was walking along the jungle road towards the meeting-pool
hen I saw it,' said the Bamboo-rat.

'I'm hungry,' yawned the Python, waking up after his long
leep. 'What news, my brother?'

'Good hunting,' cried the Stick Insect. 'Look what's coming
long the jungle road!'

All the animals stopped their whispering, rustling, and
umbling and looked along the jungle road.

A silence fell in the grass and the trees. Not a leaf stirred. The
tick Insect stood stock-still looking just like the twig it was
tanding on, and the Slow Loris' two eyes stared down from the
pper branches of the tapang tree like two bright lamps. The
Flying-fox hung upside down with her head between her
houlders looking like a bundle of dried bark, and the Pig hid
imself in the lalang grass. The Python lay coiled around his
ough, his wicked head hanging down over the jungle road; and
p above him, the long soft nose and the little black eyes of
Bruang the Bear stuck out of his tree-hole.

The White Man's child came walking along under the trees
ucking his thumb and looking at the fireflies. Every now and
hen he pulled his thumb out of his mouth and made a grab at
hem and laughed because he couldn't catch them.

Under the tapang tree the White Man's child stopped. He
could see the two great eyes of the Slow Loris and he thought

they must be a new and splendid kind of firefly.

'Now's your chance,' whispered the Stick Insect to the Python. 'You'll never get another like it.'

'I don't know,' whispered the Python uneasily. 'I don't like the look of it. It might be a trap. I swallowed a monkey once, and a human had put a hook inside it, and I was six weeks digesting it.'

'Bunkum!' whispered the Stick Insect excitedly. 'There's no trap about it. Go on! Get rid of the White Man's cub and it will frighten the White Man away, and we shall have our island to ourselves.'

'Yes, yes,' whispered all the other animals, and their voices just stirred the grass and the leaves like a tiny breeze. 'Get rid of the White Man's cub and we get rid of the White Man too!'

The White Child did not hear the whispering in the trees and the grass. He was laughing at the fireflies and sucking his thumb.

'Quick,' whispered the Stick Insect. 'Strike now!'

The Python looked away along the jungle road and at the White Man's child, and drew back his head to strike.

'Now we've got him,' screamed the Stick Insect, forgetting everything in his excitement; but at that moment, before the Python could reach the child, Bruang the Bear threw himself out of his hole right on top of the Python's back and drove his long curved claws and his forty-three long white teeth into his neck.

'Help, help!' yelled the Stick Insect. 'Pull him off, some one! He's a friend of the White Man and he's spoiling everything!'

But none of the other animals felt a bit like interfering. They just crept well out of the way up the trees and looked on.

It was the most tremendous fight the jungle creatures had ever seen. Up and down and to and fro the Python lashed his wicked

ead. He banged and banged and banged it on the ground. He
ammered it against the tree-trunks. He whirled it round and
ound in a circle, beating the grass flat and bringing the leaves and
ranches down in showers from the trees. But the little bear hung
n. His four paws and his forty-three white teeth were so deep in
ne Python's neck that nothing could shake them out unless he let
o himself; but his little eyes were shut and he was growling to
imself 'I've been and gone and done it! I *must* hold on! I *can't*
et go now!'

Then the Python thought he would try to drown the bear.
nto the meeting-pool he flung himself, scattering the frogs and
he calling-crabs far and wide. Round and round the meeting-
ool he rushed till the water foamed and frothed and spurted like
water-spout.

But the little bear held on.

'I've got this far now – I'll *have* to see it through,' he muttered
etween his forty-three clenched teeth.

Then the Python, quite silly now with pain and rage and fear,
ushed past the little boy, nearly knocking him over with a swish
f his tail, and tore off into the jungle, smashing everything down
hat stood in his way; but it wasn't long before he came tearing
ack again, and there was the little bear still clinging to his neck.

'It can't last *much* longer,' the little bear was growling to him-
elf. 'one of us has *got* to stop and I *hope* it won't be me!'

Off the Python rushed into the jungle and back he rushed
gain. The little bear was feeling sick and giddy, and he was
orribly bruised and battered, but he clung on just the same.

'Oh, oh!' shouted the Stick Insect. 'If only some one would
top the fight before the White Cub runs away.'

But nobody was brave enough to stop the fight, and quite a lot of the animals hoped the bear would win. The python's struggle got weaker and weaker and his head sank lower and lower, and at last he died. Bruang the Bear still had his four sets of claws and his forty-three sharp teeth in the Python's neck, but he was dead too, for the Python had got two coils of his body round him at last and had crushed the life right out of him.

Just then the animals heard something rushing down the jungle road.

'Look out,' cried the Stick Insect in a terrified voice. 'Here comes the White Man!'

THE
LAST
MEETING

THE LAST MEETING

AT WHICH THE WHITE MAN TELLS A STORY

'GOODNESS!' said the Mosquito, buzzing up to the meeting-pool the next evening. 'What's the matter with you all? You look as if you'd swallowed something that didn't agree with you.'

'It's all very well for you to talk,' said the Slow Loris gloomily. 'It doesn't matter to you if the White Man does clear the jungle, but what's going to happen to us?'

'That's right,' said the Ape. 'Now that the Python's killed the Bear and the Bear's killed the Python, the White Man is lord of the jungle and he will do what he likes with us.'

'It was all the fault of Bruang,' said the Stick Insect, 'poking his nose in where he had no business to!'

'The White Man's magic is stronger than our magic,' said the Slow Loris. 'Why, even his cub is braver than we are. Did you see how it laughed and clapped its hands while the Python and the Bear were fighting?'

'And did you see how the White Man picked it up and licked its face and threw it in the air and then carried it off on his shoulder, and it laughed all the time?' said the Flying-fox.

'Well,' said the Mosquito. 'What are you going to do about it?'

'I shall fly across to Borneo,' said Rawa the big white pigeon.

'I suppose,' squeaked Babi the Pig, looking cautiously up and down the beach to see if the Crocodile was anywhere within hearing, 'I suppose I shall have to swim.'

'You might let me know when you're going to start,' squattered the Buffalo-leech, hooping himself along towards the Pig. 'I'd like to take a passage with you. I promise not to suck your blood until we get to the other side.'

'What's going to hapen to me?' whimpered the Stick Insect. 'I can't swim and I can't fly – not that distance at anyrate.'

'You'll get cooked when the White Man burns the last bit of jungle,' jeered the Mosquito, 'and serve you right! You always did have too much to say.'

The fireflies had been listening, and in their terror at the thought of being burnt up, they snapped their lamps on and off so quickly that the screwpine they were lodging in was lighted up just as if a stray beam of sunshine had got left behind, after the sun had sunk, and had got caught in the branches.

'What a lovely sight,' said a voice that few of the jungle people had ever heard before. 'Look how that tree is reflected in the pool!'

All the animals looked round in a fright.

'Green leaves and twigs,' whispered the Stick Insect. 'Here comes the White Man!'

'And his wife,' squeaked the Pig.

'Yes,' said the Flying-fox, 'and there's a nurse, too. bringing the White Man's cub.'

'I hope they're not going to put a magic on us,' whimpered the Slow Loris, blinking his big round eyes.

'Perhaps,' stuttered the Pig, 'he is going to give us all to his cub to eat.'

'Sh-sh!' squattered the Buffalo-leech. 'The White Man's talking. Let's listen to what he's got to say.'

'Yes,' the White Man was saying, 'I'm very fond of this patch of forest. It is the last bit of bush left on the island. It was just over there, on the edge of the pool, underneath that tapang tree, that I found our boy. He was standing just here,' and the White Man walked up the beach, while all the animals scampered silently back into the jungle. 'The Python was lying there, just a few feet away, stone-dead, and the young Bear was stone-dead too, with its teeth burried in the Python's neck. It was the same little Bear I saved from the Python a year ago and brought up in the house. I knew it by the white horseshoe-mark on its chest.'

'It was a wonderful escape for our boy,' murmured the White Man's wife.

'It was,' said the White Man. 'Wonderful. And for that reason, if for no other, I don't think I'll clear away this bit of bush. After all, rubber-trees are not everything, and I daresay there are birds, animals, and even insects in this little patch of jungle that are worth preserving.'

'My leaves and twigs,' whispered the Stick Insect, indignantly. 'I should just about say there were!'

'I should like to think,' went on the White Man, sitting down at the edge of the meeting-pool, 'that this patch of jungle was a haven of refuge for all the animals in it, as the bendoo-tree was to the white ants.'

'Are you going to tell us a story, Dad?' asked the White Man's child, climbing on to his father's knee.

'Yes, if you don't fidget or yawn,' laughed the White Man. 'It's called

THE TREE WITH THE SOFTEST HEART.'

THE TREE

WITH THE SOFTEST HEART

THE TREE WITH THE SOFTEST HEART

HAVE you ever seen a white ant, began the White Man, while all the jungle people crowded down as close as they dared to listen. I don't expect you have, because they are not a bit fond of the light, and live, if they can, inside the hearts of trees.

White ants don't like trees with hard or nasty-smelling wood; they only like the soft and sweet-smelling ones. But there is one tree whose wood is soft and sweet and yet the white ants never touch it, and it is called the bendoo-tree. And this is why the white ants never try to eat the bendoo-tree.

Once upon a time there was a great flood. It rained and rained until the water began to rise over the tops of the houses and over the tops of the trees. It frightened the white ants and they started from their homes under the houses to see if they could get away from the water by climbing up into the hills. But the water rose higher and higher and began to creep up the hills too. So the white ants became really frightened they would be drowned. There was nowhere they could get away from the water but up in the tallest trees. They went up to all the trees they knew and asked them if they could climb up into their branches for a while until the rain stopped and the water went down. First they went to the jambu-tree, but when he saw these millions and millions of hungry mouths moving towards him, he trembled all over and said, 'No thanks, I don't want to be eaten to-day! Go and try my friend the bilian-tree. He has much better accommodation than I have.'

'But we promise on our honour not to eat you,' said the millions of white ants.

'Who ever heard of white ants having any honour,' sneered the jambu-tree, turning his nose up at them, 'go and try that story on my next-door neighbour.'

So the white ants went off to his next-door neighbour, the bilian-tree, and asked him the same question.

'Not on your sweet life,' said the bilian-tree, scowling at them fiercely, 'go and ask the waru-tree there, over the way.'

The white ants were getting tired and they hated being kept out in the light so long, so they hurried to the waru-tree and asked him if *he* would give them shelter.

'Not likely,' said he, turning pale with fright at the very thought, 'I don't want to die yet, my friends! Try the waringin-tree up the hill there. He has a softer heart than mine.'

But as soon as the waringin-tree saw them coming, he began to throw his arms about with rage and bellowed at them so terribly that they ran away without even asking him to help them.

And just as they were beginning to give up hope and thought that they would all be drowned, they came to the bendoo-tree; and when they had told him their trouble, the bendoo-tree, who had the softest heart of all the trees, said, 'Well, if you will all promise not to hurt me or any of my family for the rest of our lives, you can come up into my branches until the water has gone down.'

They all promised quickly enough, and so then he let them climb up his big smooth trunk and shelter in his hair; and next day the rain stopped and the water had gone down, so they all climbed down again and went to their homes in the foundations of the houses; but they kept their promise, and never have they touched the bendoo-tree from that day to this. But the other trees they eat as often as they can. That is why the people always build their houses of the wood of the bendoo-tree whenever they can get it.

'And now,' said the White Man, putting down the boy so suddenly that all the jungle creatures scampered hastily farther back into the shadows, 'it's time children were in bed. It will be too black soon to see our way home along the beach. Did you hear that rustling in the grass? I wouldn't be surprised if quite a

t of eyes were watching us and wondering what kind of queer
nimals we are.'

He jumped up and swung the boy on to his shoulder, but
aused a moment to gaze around him with a proud look in his
es. From where they stood they could see right across the
land, over the hills that had just been cleared, over the hills
at had not long been planted with young seedlings, to the hills
here the older rubber-trees marched straight and strong down
to the valleys and up again like regiments of soldiers.

'There's a fine sight for you,' laughed the White Man. 'Well,
ome we go! To-morrow I'll tell Amit there's to be no more
earing of the jungle.'

THE END

THE
END

THE MAGIC PUDDING

Norman Lindsay

HIS is a very funny book, about a very peculiar pudding. In pite of the word 'magic' in the title, there are no fairies or pells. Only a pudding.

Sometimes it was a rich odoriferous steak-and-kidney udding, sometimes it was boiled jam roll or apple dumpling. ll you had to do was whistle twice, turn the pudding round, nd you could have whatever you wanted! Indeed, the pudding as such a prize that there were 'professional puddin'-owners' nd, alas, 'professional puddin'-thieves'. One of the owners as Sam Sawnoff, whose feet were sitting down while his body as standing (he was a penguin), although Bill was just an rdinary small man with a large hat. The pudding had his own iews, and was apt to sing in a very gruff voice:

> O, who would be a puddin',
> A puddin' in a pot,
> A puddin' which is stood on
> A fire which is hot?
> O sad indeed the lot
> Of puddin's in a pot.

or ages eight to eighty, allowing for brief blind periods now nd again in between.

AN OLDER KIND OF MAGIC

Patricia Wrightson

Beneath the earth are older things than perhaps we understand, as old as the ground in which they live, and part of it. Every so often, when the time is right, they appear again above the earth to visit the world that once was theirs alone.

Greg knew the comet was coming: Selina, Rupert and Benny knew as well but they didn't wait for its arrival with the same sense of excitement and wonder. They had other things on their minds; for by chance they had overheard the meeting at which Sir Mortimer Wyvern suggested taking part of the Botanic Gardens to build a new car park. The gardens belonged to everyone and the children were determined to prevent even part of them from being destroyed. Sir Mortimer was powerful and used to having his own way but, luckily, the children had all the help they needed. Not only the Minister and bearded Ernest Hawke but other, stranger, allies! And all the time the comet grew closer, bringing with it its own special brand of magic.

An Older Kind of Magic is a modern Australian fantasy by the author of *The Rocks of Honey* and *Down to Earth*. It was highly commended by the judges of the Children's Book Council of Australia Book of the Year Awards in 1973.

For readers who like adventure and mystery.